WHO WILL BELL THE CAT?

PATRICIA C. McKISSACK

ILLUSTRATED BY

CHRISTOPHER CYR

HOLIDAY HOUSE • NEW YORK

FOR MY FRIEND MOUSE, WISE MOUSE, AND MARMALADE
—C.C.

Text copyright © 2018 by Patricia C. McKissack   Illustrations copyright © 2018 by Christopher Cyr
All Rights Reserved   HOLIDAY HOUSE is registered in the U.S. Patent and Trademark Office.
Printed and bound in November 2017 at Hong Kong Graphics and Printing Ltd., China.   The artwork was created with digital tools.
www.holidayhouse.com   First Edition   1 3 5 7 9 10 8 6 4 2
Library of Congress Cataloging-in-Publication Data is available.   ISBN 978-0-8234-3700-9

The barn mice decided that if they put a bell around the cat's neck, they would know where she was at all times. Good idea, but who was going to bell the cat?

O N an icy winter evening a large tabby cat named Marmalade stumbled into the barn—cold, sick, and hungry.

The mice took pity on the cat. They made her a warm bed of straw, shared their food and water, and nursed her back to health.

As soon as Marmalade felt better she began terrorizing the mice—chasing, threatening, and making their lives miserable. She was a horror.

"Why are you doing this to us?" the mice cried.

"You knew I was a cat when you let me in," Marmalade replied with a wicked growl. "I'm simply doing what cats do—chasing mice!"

"We must stop Marmalade," Smart Mouse said at
the mouse meeting. "We have lived in this barn for
generations. We can't let one cat destroy our home.
We must defend ourselves."

The other mice erupted into cheers and applause.

"Who will join me?" Smart Mouse asked.

Friend Mouse stepped forward.

With no warning, Marmalade leaped into the middle of the meeting. Large and small, young and old, the mice scattered to the far corners of the barn.

"We've got to do something soon," said Smart Mouse when everyone was safe.

"But what can we do against a foe like Marmalade?" Friend Mouse asked.

Wise Mouse, the oldest member of the community, stepped forward. "Whatever you do is going to be dangerous. Marmalade is a formidable enemy."

Smart Mouse was foraging outside the barn when she stumbled upon some sleigh bells. She chewed one off and then hurried to find her friend.

"I've got a solution to our cat problem," Smart Mouse announced, holding up the bell. "We'll make a collar and put it around Marmalade's neck. She'll never be able to sneak up on us again."

"It might just work," said Friend Mouse. "Let's get started."

For weeks, the two mice worked. They cut a leather band from an old saddlebag and pulled the band through the bell hoop.

The mice made a knot at one end of the leather band and used a nail to make a hole at the other end. Done! It was a perfect collar, tailor-made for Marmalade.

Smart Mouse and Friend Mouse took the collar to the next monthly mouse meeting.

But once again, Wise Mouse stepped up. "You two are to be commended for all your hard work, but who among us will take on the dangerous challenge of belling the cat?"

The first plan seemed a sure bet. Smart Mouse
found the perfect volunteers: the triplets, three of the
smallest mice in the barn—Wee Mouse, Tiny Mouse,
and Teeny Mouse.

Friend Mouse tied them to some fishing line
and slowly lowered them just above the napping
Marmalade when . . .

. . . Teeny Mouse let go a very loud sneeze! *Achoo!*
Marmalade's eyes opened wide! She lashed out at the
dangling mice.

"Help!" they screamed.

Friend Mouse quickly pulled them in and away to safety.

"All I did was make matters worse," Smart Mouse said sadly.

But Friend Mouse was *not* discouraged. "We can't give up now," Friend Mouse said. "How about seeking help from the Rat Pack?"

"Them?" shouted Smart Mouse, amazed that her friend would consider such a thing.

"Desperate times require desperate plans," Friend Mouse said.

Smart Mouse agreed. Off they went to the junk heap to
meet with the rats, a disagreeable, unkempt breed of rodent
that created chaos and confusion wherever they went.
Their nasty dispositions matched their arrogance and greed.

Though uncomfortable, Smart Mouse kept her composure
as she spoke to Head Rat. "We need your help to put a bell
around the neck of our bitter enemy, a cat!"

"What's in it for us?" Head Rat asked.

"Name your price."

"We need clean, dry straw to make our beds warm and toasty,
like yours."

"If you help us, we will gladly share our straw with you. Done
deal," Friend Mouse said.

The Rat Pack attacked in full force while the barn mice stayed well hidden. Ten of the biggest, meanest rats anyone could imagine swooped down on Marmalade, who was caught off guard.

No matter. Instantly, the rats realized they were no match for this fierce feline.

She was everywhere at once—hissing and snarling, leaping, pouncing, fur flying. Marmalade hurled the rats one by one against the wall, out the door, into buckets and baskets. She bit and tore at their fur, scratched and bruised their legs and heads.

As Head Rat and his gang fled the barn, he promised never to go there again.

"Keep the straw," he shouted.

For weeks thereafter, Marmalade continued to terrify the mice. Smart Mouse and Friend Mouse kept coming up with ideas to bell her, but nothing worked. In fact, Marmalade had just made a feast of a barn bird who had tried to help the mice.

The two mice friends were thinking about what they might
do next when a truck pulled up. Four giants got out of the car
and hurried into the house that had been abandoned for years.

Humans! The mice had never seen any but they had heard
stories about how dangerous humans were.

The smallest giant took an interest in the barn and Marmalade. The human creature didn't appear to be mean or unkind. Just different. And so big!

"Remember," said Friend Mouse. "We are to stay clear of the humans. They aren't known to be friendly toward mice."

"We don't need to be friends with the humans to get their help!" Smart Mouse's ears stood up the way they did when she had an idea. She ran to the loft, leaned over, and dropped the collar on the floor in front of the giant.

The human saw the collar and picked it up.

"Oh, look, kitty cat," she said, smiling. "A collar with a bell on it. Just perfect for you." She fastened the collar around the cat's neck. "Now, I'll always know where you are."

"And so will we," said the mice.

But old Wise Mouse shook his head. "When you use a tiger to get rid of a lion, what will you do with the tiger?

"Oh, well," he added with resolve. "That's another problem for a different day."